Just Like You

 ZONDER**kidz**

ZONDERVAN.com/
AUTHORTRACKER
follow your favorite authors

written by Marla Stewart Konrad
illustrated by Lin Wang

For Nathan, Aidan, and Juliana.
Each of you knows ... I always dreamed of someone
just like you.

—MK

To my daughter Megan and my son Nicholas.

—LW

ZONDERKIDZ

Just Like You
Copyright © 2010 by Marla Stewart Konrad
Illustrations © 2010 by Lin Wang

Requests for information should be addressed to:

Zondervan, *Grand Rapids, Michigan 49530*

Library of Congress Cataloging-in-Publication Data
Konrad, Marla Stewart
    Just like you / by Marla Stewart Konrad
       p. cm.
    Summary: A loving mother tells about the special day her child was born and
how on that same day around the world many other children were born and
celebrated in a unique way.
      ISBN 978-0-310-71478-1 (hardcover-jacketed printed)
      [1. Babies—Fiction 2. Mother and child—Fiction.] I. Title.
  PZ7.K835515Ju 2010
  [E]—2–dc22
                                                        2008036124

All Scripture quotations, unless otherwise indicated, are taken from the Holy Bible,
New International Version®, NIV®. Copyright © 1973, 1978, 1984 by Biblica, Inc.™
Used by permission of Zondervan. All rights reserved worldwide.

Any Internet addresses (websites, blogs, etc.) and telephone numbers printed in
this book are offered as a resource. They are not intended in any way to be or imply
an endorsement by Zondervan, nor does Zondervan vouch for the content of these
sites and numbers for the life of this book.

Editor: Barbara Herndon
Art direction and design: Sarah Molegraaf

Printed in China

10 11 12 13 14 /LPC/ 6 5 4 3 2 1

I originally began writing *Just Like You* to express all the love and joy I felt when each of my children was born. But suddenly, the little story about my family grew, and I found myself writing about families from all over the world.

As I continued writing, another theme emerged: that while we may not look like one another, and while our cultures and customs are miles apart, the one thing we have in common is the love of family, especially that special bond between a mother and her newborn baby.

I've had the opportunity to live and travel overseas, and through many years of working with World Vision, I've met families just like these. Many struggle to provide the basics of life for their children, and for that reason some of the royalties from this book will be invested in children's lives through World Vision.

I hope this book cultivates special moments in your family. Tonight, when you tuck your child in, remind them how much God loves them and all the children of the world. And be sure to tell them—the world has been waiting for someone... just like you.

Marla Stewart Konrad

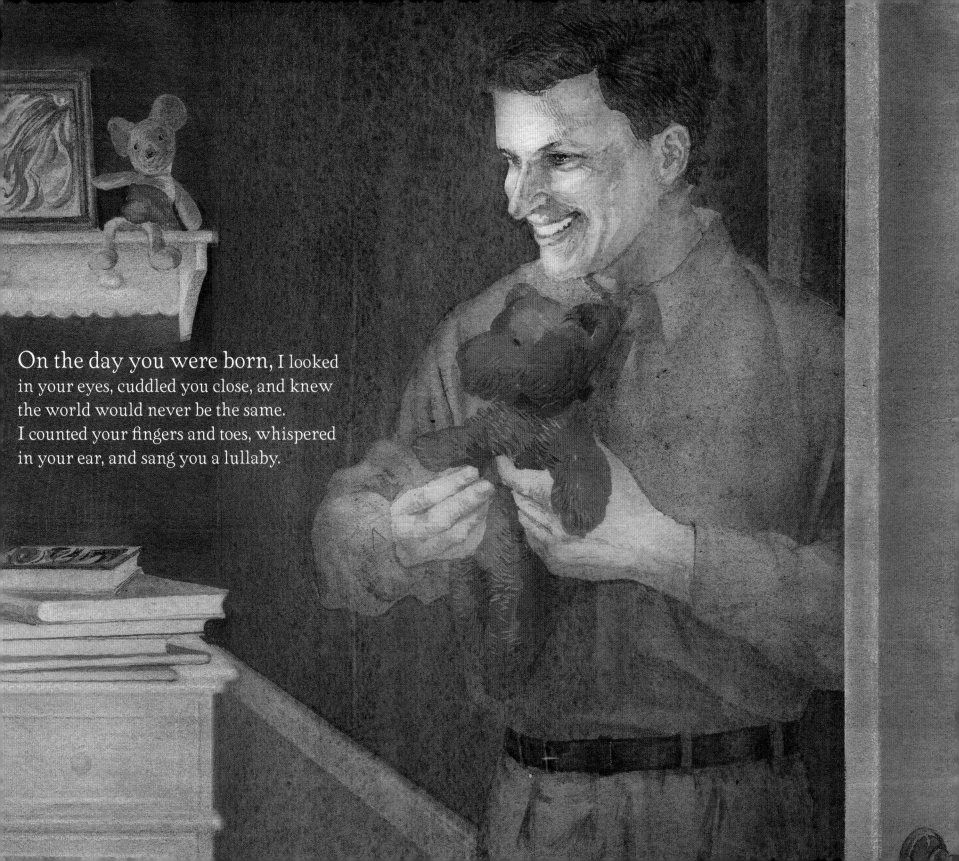

On the day you were born, I looked
in your eyes, cuddled you close, and knew
the world would never be the same.
I counted your fingers and toes, whispered
in your ear, and sang you a lullaby.

Grandma and Grandpa came to see you
and brought you a tinkling rattle and a fat snowsuit.
Your auntie came by and brought some baby soap
for you and a hot casserole for me—to fatten me up
again, she said.

When I tucked you in that first night, all the
stars of the universe sparkled through your window.

You closed your eyes, stretched your arms wide, and went to
sleep. I closed my eyes, stretched my arms wide, and I thought
I could hug the whole world.

You were everything I wanted, because I wanted a baby... just like you.

On the day you were born, baby Mei Ling was born in China. Her mommy looked in her eyes and cuddled her close. She counted her fingers and toes, whispered in her ear, and sang her a lullaby.

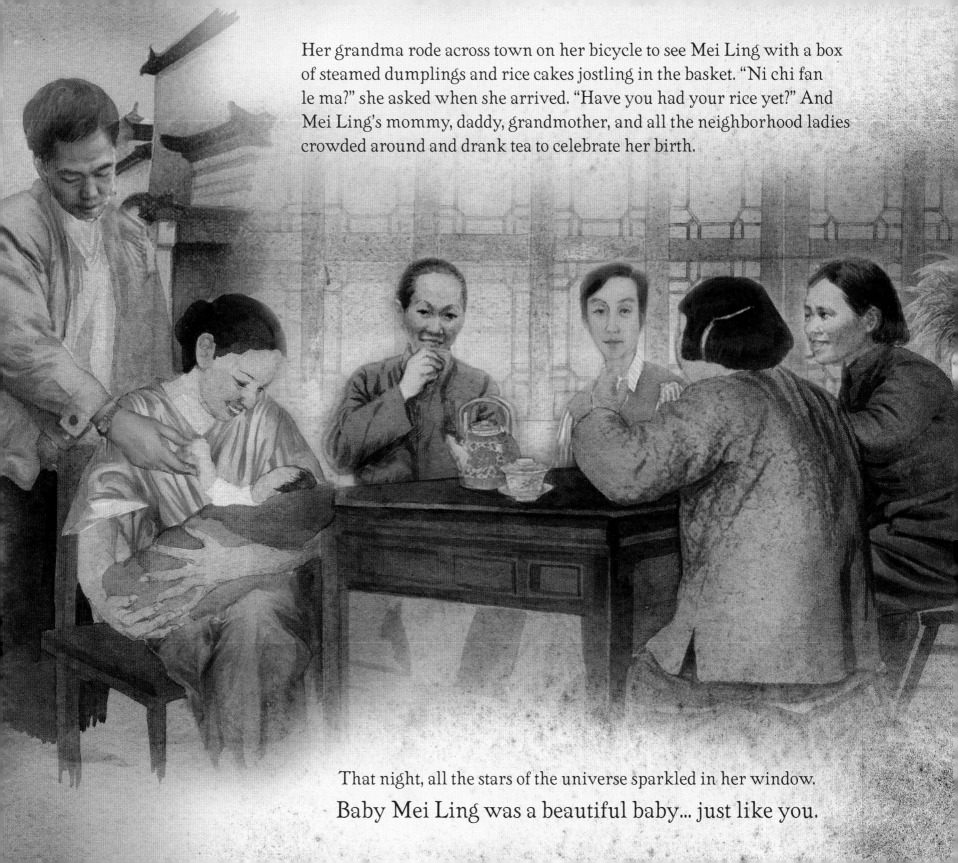

Her grandma rode across town on her bicycle to see Mei Ling with a box of steamed dumplings and rice cakes jostling in the basket. "Ni chi fan le ma?" she asked when she arrived. "Have you had your rice yet?" And Mei Ling's mommy, daddy, grandmother, and all the neighborhood ladies crowded around and drank tea to celebrate her birth.

That night, all the stars of the universe sparkled in her window.
Baby Mei Ling was a beautiful baby... just like you.

On the day you were born, baby Carlos was born in the Amazon rain forest. His mommy looked in his eyes and cuddled him close. She counted his fingers and toes, whispered in his ear, and sang him a lullaby.

His grandfather is the chief of the village, so all of the neighbors brought presents—fish from the river and fruit from the forest. His sister took a hollow gourd and brought water from the well to wash him. His grandmother laid him in a hammock under the shade trees to keep him cool.

That night, all the stars of the universe sparkled through those shade trees.
Baby Carlos was a beautiful baby... just like you.

On the day you were born, baby Sofia was born in Russia. Her mommy looked in her eyes and cuddled her close. She counted her fingers and toes, whispered in her ear, and sang her a lullaby.

The cousins who came to see her loved the elevator ride up, up, up to the twentieth floor. Marina brought her a velvet hair ribbon. Alexandra wrapped up her favorite pink ballet slippers that did not fit her anymore. Peter brought her five little nesting dolls, one inside the other.

That night, all the stars of the universe sparkled through the windows of the apartment.

Baby Sofia was a beautiful baby... just like you.

On the day you were born, baby Amaruq was born in the Arctic.
His mommy looked in his eyes and cuddled him close. She counted his
fingers and toes, whispered in his ear, and sang him a lullaby.

In the cold evening, the family gathered around a crackling fire and ate caribou stew while Grandfather told a story. Even the dogs stopped barking when he talked about snow houses and riding in kayaks to hunt whales. Baby Amaruq's mother wrapped him in blankets of fur and kissed his tiny head.

That night, all the stars of the universe sparkled across the snow and through the windows of the wooden house.
Baby Amaruq was a beautiful baby... just like you.

On the day you were born, baby Samer was born in Egypt. His mommy looked in his eyes and cuddled him close. She counted his fingers and toes, whispered in his ear, and sang him a lullaby.

The cousins came by with their arms full of gifts. The aunts and uncles carried baskets brimming with vegetables and rice and sticky sweets. While the children laughed and danced in circles, baby Samer slept and slept.

That night when the party was over, all the stars of the universe sparkled through the window.
Baby Samer was a beautiful baby...
just like you.

On the day you were born, baby Kitoto was born in southern Africa. Her mommy looked in her eyes and cuddled her close. She counted her fingers and toes, whispered in her ear, and sang her a lullaby.

All of her family crowded around in the bright sunshine to see little Kitoto wrapped in brightly woven cloth. The boys chased away the goats and the sheep when they came too close, and the girls gave baby Kitoto little necklaces and earrings they had made with colorful beads.

That night, all the stars of the universe sparkled through the door of the little mud home.

Baby Kitoto was a beautiful baby... just like you.

On the day you were born, baby Vijay was born in India. His mommy looked in his eyes and cuddled him close. She counted his fingers and toes, whispered in his ear, and sang him a lullaby.

Vijay's daddy tugged his fishing boat up onto the sand and ran home with nine fat fish for supper. His grandmother raced to the market to buy a bag of rice and sweets for the entire family. After supper, all of the aunts and uncles and cousins who lived in the big white house gathered outside in the cool of the evening to take a peek at the tiny new life.

That night, all the stars of the universe sparkled through the palm trees in that busy yard.

Baby Vijay was a beautiful baby... just like you.

On the day you were born, baby Coorah was born in Australia. Her mommy looked in her eyes and cuddled her close. She counted her fingers and toes, whispered in her ear, and sang her a lullaby.

Under the gum trees, the lullaby woke up a baby koala who peered out from its mother's pouch. A frilled lizard opened a sleepy eye and fluttered his scaly red frill. A parrot squawked and woke up the kookaburras who then started to laugh. And, for a moment, the quiet countryside had a noisy celebration.

That night, all the stars of the universe sparkled through those silvery white gum trees.

Baby Coorah was a beautiful baby... just like you.

On the day you were born, God wrapped his gentle arms around the whole world. He looked into the eyes of every tiny baby and laid them in their mothers' arms. He counted the hairs on each little head.

And he called the angels to sing a lullaby of joy.

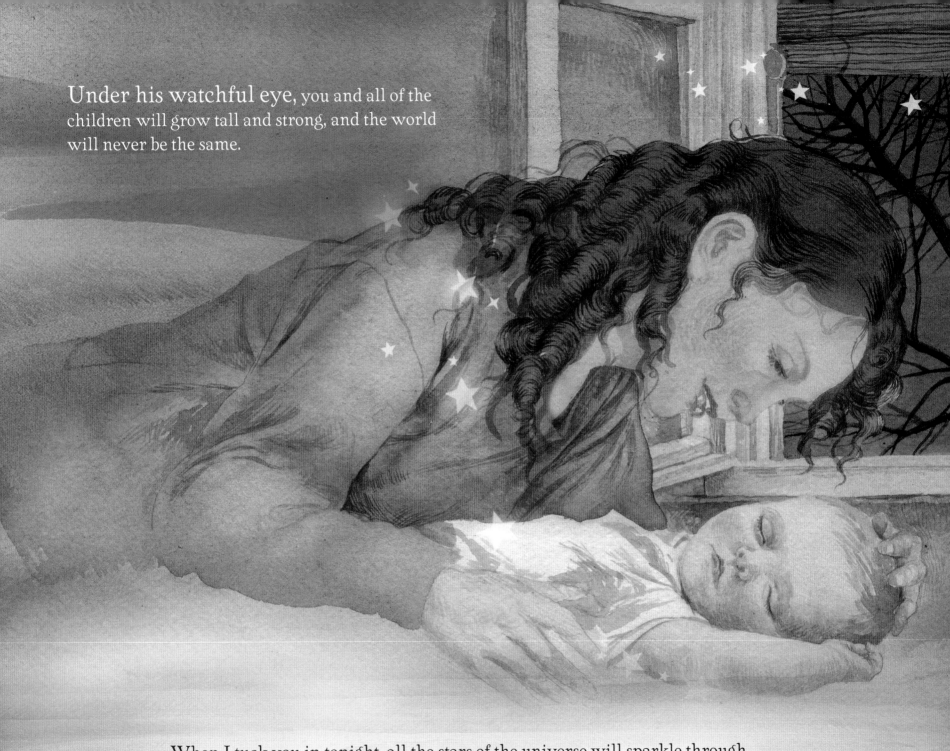

Under his watchful eye, you and all of the children will grow tall and strong, and the world will never be the same.

When I tuck you in tonight, all the stars of the universe will sparkle through your window. I'll close my eyes and thank God for his special gift to me.

You were everything I wanted, because I wanted a baby... just like you.